An Olde Christmas Carol

A Storm Ketchum Tale

by

Garrett Dennis

TBD Press, Binghamton NY

Copyright © 2015 by Garrett Dennis. All rights reserved under International and Pan-American Copyright Conventions. No part of this text may be reproduced in any form or by any means without the express written permission of the author.

This story is a work of fiction. The Kinnakeet Boatyard and the Sea Dog Scuba Center are fictitious. Other businesses and organizations, locales, scientific and religious references, and historical figures and events are real, but may be used fictitiously.

AN OLDE CHRISTMAS CAROL
Storm Ketchum Tale #1
ISBN: 978-1514897690

~ Author's Note ~

Greetings, and welcome to my world! I'm the author of the **Storm Ketchum Adventures** series of cozy Outer Banks mysteries, which begins with the full-length novel ***Port Starbird***.

The short story you're about to read is meant to serve as both an introduction and a companion to that series, and can be read along with or independently of the books in the series.

For more about the series, please visit **www.GarrettDennis.com** . That site also contains information on how to connect with me on social media and by e-mail.

And now – sit back and enjoy!

~ An Olde Christmas Carol ~

Ketch gingerly eased himself into the rickety old rocking chair on the front porch. It held, so he draped the afghan he'd dragged outside with him across his lap. Although he was fully dressed and the temperature here on Cape Hatteras was nowhere near as low on this early January morning as it had been back North where he'd come from, that number alone was deceptive. There was no snow on the ground, but he was surrounded by water, so the air here was always damp – and when the sea breezes blew, it was just as capable of chilling one to the bone as an upstate New York winter.

Jack didn't appear to be bothered by the weather, but Ketch figured that could be due to the dog's interest in the plate of buttered toast he'd set on a nearby stand. The two-year-old beagle-lab mix he'd rescued from a shelter a few months back on a whim was already intensely loyal, and unexpectedly well-behaved and atypically polite (for a dog) when it came to food. He didn't think he'd ever before met a dog as intelligent and empathetic as this one.

Though he wasn't looking for friends, Ketch appreciated the dog's silent camaraderie, and more saliently the calming effect the dog's presence seemed to have had on his own fevered mind, something the human therapist he'd grudgingly engaged for a time hadn't been able to achieve. Ketch fed Jack a well-deserved slice of toast before digging in himself on the remaining two. He saved the last crust for the dog and then washed his breakfast down with a glass of orange juice.

He was still cold, so he stood and wrapped the afghan around himself like one would a bath towel, then sat back down. It probably didn't help that he was hungover. Contrary to popular tales of alpine rescues, and in spite of the false burn it created on the way down, alcohol lowered the body's core temperature and wasn't really an effective way to get or stay warm. It also didn't permanently solve any problems, a fact he'd always known but had lately chosen to ignore. The dog, satisfied now, curled up on the throw rug under Ketch's stockinged feet and allowed them to rest on his back.

Warmer now, Ketch sat back and took in the view this Buxton cottage provided. Though it wasn't a waterfront property, he could make out the Cape Hatteras lighthouse with its distinctive black-and-white barbershop-pole day marker in the dawning sun and hear the breakers from here. Since this was just a relatively inexpensive ninety-day rental whose purpose was to shelter him and Jack while he house-hunted in Avon, and since he was finally on his beloved Hatteras Island for good regardless of anything else, that was enough for him.

For the first time in as long as he could remember, there was nothing he absolutely had to do today. Although the thirty-first was his official retirement date, he'd been able to take the Christmas holidays and this entire month off due to accrued vacation time. He'd already sold his old house, and the few belongings he'd decided to keep were in a self-storage unit not too far away. And he'd shopped at Conner's grocery after checking in here, so he had adequate provisions – which was good, since this island's economy was predominantly tourism-driven these days and the restaurants were all closed off-season. And he didn't have enough laundry to bother with.

So what should he do today, with this bounty of free time – drink some more? No, he thought not, though he still felt justified in considering it. Maybe play a little more guitar and then do a bit of beachcombing after the temperature had risen some, or perhaps a mini-hike through part of the nearby Buxton Woods Reserve? It was the largest remaining stand of maritime forest on the Outer Banks, and its trails extended all the way south to Frisco. The reptiles and insects there wouldn't be too troublesome at this time of year.

He remembered reading that there was a trailhead not far from here, near the small cemetery past the lighthouse. The British Cemetery held the graves of two sailors from across the pond whose bodies had washed ashore after their vessel was torpedoed by one of the German U-boats that prowled the East Coast during World War II. He'd always meant to visit there, but had never gotten around to it on his previous visits to the island. Well, he had plenty of time to do that now, and more.

He also knew today was a Christmas of sorts and there'd be a celebration of that up in Rodanthe, as there was every year. But although that did admittedly pique his interest from a cultural perspective, a tranquil day by the sea with his always accommodating canine companion was more appealing at the moment. There'd probably be a lot of people at that shindig, and he'd had enough of people.

He'd never himself attended despite numerous vacations taken on this island, but Ketch knew from his readings that Old Christmas, or Olde Christmas to the more nostalgic, was a holiday born of miscommunication and stubbornness, and maintained as much out of winter island boredom as tradition. The story was, the Pope decreed in 1582 that the inaccurate Julian calendar be replaced by our modern Gregorian calendar. The Catholic European nations went along, but by the time Protestant England came around, almost two hundred years had passed and there was an eleven-day difference between the two calendars that had to be dealt with.

Before the Calendar Act of 1751, England had celebrated Christmas on January 6, a practice begun in medieval times. Dropping the extra eleven days moved Christmas back to December 25. By their nature resistant to change, the people of the isolated Outer Banks communities initially ignored the new date when they heard about it several years later, and continued to celebrate on January 6.

Then, realizing the potential for additional partying, to which they were always amenable, the Banker colonists decided to extend their holiday. They started observing both the 'official' Christmas on

December 25, and what came to be called Old Christmas on January 6. On Hatteras Island nowadays, folks congregated at the community center (which the locals simply referred to as the community building) in Rodanthe on the Saturday closest to that day each year to celebrate Old Christmas.

Ketch wasn't a religious man, and Christmas had never really meant that much to him even in the secular sense after his wife and son had moved on and left him behind. But Old Christmas wasn't a religious event, and since he desired to know his new island home and its history as intimately as possible, he supposed he should experience it at some point – but he'd just stay put here for today, he again decided. Having no family left to speak of now, his traditional Christmas had been a solitary affair, and he didn't see why this particular day needed to be any different. Maybe next year...

The temperature had risen a bit now, and he found he was quite comfortable under the afghan. The fur-coated dog seemed content as well beneath his feet. He could clearly hear the gulls down toward the beach, making their contributions to the soul-soothing cacophony that was the sound of the sea. That and the pleasantly salty air, chilly but still this morning, and the rising sun suffusing his seaside vista with the glow of the new day were all working their magic on him just as he'd remembered, and had hoped they would again. He wondered if he could maybe just close his eyes and rest here for a little while before he did whatever else he'd end up doing today – and then he realized yes, of course he could if he wanted to, why on Earth not?

~ ~ ~

Now what was that boy doing hitchhiking in this day and age? There'd been a time when Ketch might have picked him up, and when he'd thumbed a few rides himself to get home from college for a weekend, but those days were long gone. This one couldn't be more than twelve, and his clothes didn't look clean. Ketch didn't stop.

After he'd passed the boy, he couldn't help but glance back one time in the rearview mirror. But he still didn't brake. No, it was simply too risky these days. He refocused on the road ahead and left Buxton, and the boy, behind.

This was one of his favorite stretches of Highway 12, the two-lane road that ran the fifty-odd-mile length of the island. The landscape from the outskirts of Buxton north to Avon was still almost pristine, and when he approached the haulover, an especially narrow part of the slender island where the old-time Hatterasmen had once hauled their wooden boats between the sound and the sea, he'd be able to see both Pamlico Sound to his left and the Atlantic to his right.

He wasn't enjoying this ride as much as he usually did, though, maybe because a part of him wanted to turn around and pick up that poor boy. There likely wouldn't be much traffic today, since the winter population here was only a small fraction of the summer one, and who knew what that kid's personal situation was and why he was hitching in the first place? Maybe he could legitimately use a lift. But helping folks like him was what Ketch liked to call an S.E.P. – Somebody Else's Problem. Weren't there government programs and charities and such for people like that? Ketch's pickup hadn't broken down and his dog hadn't died, but otherwise he was almost a walking country-song disaster himself. He didn't have the time or the energy to worry about everyone else.

But Jack was enjoying himself, ears up and snout poking out into the olfactory feast whizzing by his half-open window. It was so easy to please a dog, easier than people, and almost always more gratifying to boot. Dogs were inarguably more transparent than people.

They reached Rodanthe in a surprisingly short time, considering it was about five miles from Buxton to Avon, and then almost another twenty after that. And with some more unspoiled scenery in between, which Ketch didn't remember consciously noticing today, oddly enough. Too much daydreaming, he supposed.

The community building was on the sound side of Route 12, across the road from the Chicamacomico Lifesaving Station. The restored station was a museum now, commemorating the heroism of the nineteenth and early twentieth century surfmen of the U.S. Lifesaving Service, and later the Coast Guard, whose job it had been to rescue shipwreck victims from the treacherous waters of what became known as the Graveyard of the Atlantic. He wanted to spend some more time there, but not today.

He pulled his truck into the parking lot of the community building, found a place to park, and let Jack out. He hoped it would be all right to bring the dog in with him, as he didn't want to leave the poor guy in the truck. He supposed he shouldn't have brought him along, but he hadn't thought about that earlier. Though Jack was exceptionally well-behaved and it wasn't really necessary, Ketch leashed him to be on the safe side. He figured seeing the dog restrained would reassure any Nervous Nellies that the wild animal was under control, and Jack didn't seem to mind.

The building was a repurposed historic schoolhouse set atop short pilings that didn't look high enough to allow the building to ride out a major storm surge. Well, maybe they'd rebuild with more freeboard if and when. As Ketch made his way toward the building, he wondered if there'd be someone taking money for admission? He didn't recall reading about how one paid for one's food and drink at this event. But he soon saw someone sitting at a long folding table with what looked like a cashbox, so that would be the first roadblock he'd have to get the dog past.

The jovial matrons at the table didn't say anything about Jack, so he guided the dog toward the playground behind the building. He could see that some people were inside, but it looked like most of the action was out here. He figured those inside were probably involved in preparing supper, which if he recalled correctly from his reading would likely feature a traditional stewed chicken dish with pie-bread. He hadn't brought anything for Jack to eat, so he'd share some of that with the dog later.

There were, of course, oysters a-plenty as well, they being one of the centerpieces of the Old Christmas celebration (the other would make its appearance after supper). Ketch and Jack had fortuitously arrived at the conclusion of the afternoon's traditional oyster shoot adjacent to the playground, and the targets from the last of several rounds were now being judged to determine who'd receive the prize for this round, which was of course a bag of oysters. Ketch was glad Jack hadn't had to weather the afternoon's squalls of gunshots, another thing he hadn't thought of when he'd loaded the dog into his truck.

There were bushels of oysters in the process now of being roasted over a fire as well. As soon as a batch was ready, the mollusks would be shoveled – literally, as in with a large flat spade – onto wooden tables and the cycle would repeat, and the people would indulge to their hearts' content through the remainder of the afternoon and evening.

Ketch was also glad he'd worn a jacket over his light sweatshirt. His dashboard thermometer had read fifty-six the last time he'd looked at it, but it was still chilly out here near the sound, as evidenced by the heavier coats and flannels worn by the natives. It was said the blood thinned down South. Whether or not that was true, it was true that the long-term residents he'd encountered couldn't tolerate cold as well as he could. But he imagined that might change after he'd lived here for some time.

Ketch got a beer for himself and Jack a bottle of water, which he poured into a Solo cup for the dog to lap from. He'd never been particularly fond of oysters in the past, but he thought he might try one of those roasted ones later. The other revelers all seemed to be enjoying them. They also seemed to mostly know one another, which jived with what he'd read about Old Christmas being a time for family and friends to gather, rather than a religious occasion. He didn't know anyone here, and he hadn't even recognized anyone in passing so far. But he had Jack, which was all he thought he really needed.

It sounded like the band was tuning up inside, so he decided to take Jack in and have a look around. Again, no one challenged the two of them.

The main hall was tastefully decorated, with festive red streamers and tiny white lights strung throughout, and an old-timey band was indeed warming up on a stage at one end of the main hall. There was already a dessert table, and the kitchen workers were starting to set out the entrees as well. There were some other people milling around, but most were still outside. Ketch claimed a couple of the folding chairs that lined the walls of the room, left Jack leashed to one of them, and picked up two plates of stew.

The band began in earnest then, which was apparently a signal as more people started filing in from outside. There was suddenly a rapidly growing food line. He and Jack had gotten in just under the wire. Ketch decided to feed the dog and give him another drink before he went to work on his own plate.

He was just about to start eating when a woman pulled up a chair uncomfortably close to his own and purposefully dropped onto it. Jack didn't seem at all alarmed, and continued to lie on the floor next to Ketch where he'd decided to settle with his pleasantly full belly. In fact, he appeared to be having trouble keeping his eyes open. Ketch took his cue from the dog and tried to politely ignore the interloper – but then she spoke his name.

"Hello, Storm," she said, in a voice that was still familiar to him even after all this time. Ketch looked up in surprise and nearly dropped his plate.

"You know I hate that name," he automatically replied. Of all the things he could have said, why in the world had he said that? He set his plate back down on Jack's empty chair and rubbed at his eyes. When he opened them again, she was still there.

"What are *you* doing here?" he blurted, turning to face her.

"Oh, I just wanted to check on you and see how you're making out. I heard you were having some problems."

Ketch was flabbergasted at this. "How would you

know anything about that," he said, "or anything about me at all? We haven't spoken in years!" About eight, to be more precise, and they'd gotten divorced before that. And they hadn't even lived in the same state after the divorce. "How did you know I'd be here? How did you get here?" he demanded in astonishment.

She smiled and ignored his questions. "So, you had something like a nervous breakdown, you retired early, and you decided to move here. I'm not surprised, I know you always loved coming here. And this, I take it, is your new therapist?" she asked, motioning to the now-slumbering dog. "How's that working for you? Are you drinking less now?"

"What?" Ketch spluttered, at a loss for words. Though the music was filling the room now, he'd heard everything she'd said quite clearly. And now he felt guilty about the cup of beer on the floor by his chair. The old anger he'd felt years ago started to rise to the surface again. How dare she?

She held up her hands. "I'm sorry. That didn't come out quite right, did it? I don't mean to criticize. That's not why I'm here."

Then why *was* she here? "Is Rollin all right?" he inquired, the anger abruptly replaced by concern. Ketch hadn't spoken with him, either, in almost all of those years.

"Oh, I'm sorry!" she said again. "I didn't mean to scare you. Don't worry, your son is fine."

Ketch breathed a sigh of relief. Then he defiantly picked up his cup and downed a healthy gulp. What did it matter what she might think about that?

"How was your Christmas this year, Ketch?" she gently asked. "Did you do anything special?" When he didn't answer right away, she answered for him. "No, you didn't. You were all alone on Christmas morning, just you and your dog. And I know you didn't go to church, and you didn't go to any parties, either, did you?" Ketch just shrugged. "Do you remember what Christmas was like years ago, when we were all still together? Here, let me help you remember." She pulled a small photo album from her purse and opened it facing him.

"Now, you wait just a minute," he started to protest. He needed to ask her something, but he didn't know quite how to put it. "Are you, er, deceased?"

She laughed. "You think I'm a ghost? Well, I'm not."

"Well, what are you then?"

"We were joined together once. I'll always be a part of you, whether you like it or not," she cryptically replied. "Now look, here's Rollin's first Christmas," she said, leafing through the album, "and his second, and here are some from the first one where he really understood what was going on. Do you remember that one?"

Ketch did remember – the joy and wonder on the boy's face, his trusting and guileless innocence, his delight at the decorations, the tree, the gifts, all of it. They'd annually made a pilgrimage to a tree farm and cut their own starting with that Christmas, for a while anyway. He remembered how the boy had looked forward to that, until Ketch had gotten too busy and decided it was too much bother.

"And look here, Ketch," she was saying. "Here are my parents, and your parents, and your friends – you used to have some back then – and some of Rollin's friends. They were important to him, you know, since he didn't have any brothers or sisters, and not even any cousins. But one is enough, and kids adjust when you make them move to new places, right Ketch?"

Ketch was finding it increasingly difficult to speak. This was getting downright hurtful. "Why are you doing this to me?" he finally managed to eke out.

"I was sorry to hear about your father passing last year, by the way," she went on. "And so soon after your mother. I always liked them." She flipped another page. "Look at these now. Do you notice anything odd about them?" Ketch obeyed, but he couldn't discern anything out of the ordinary. "You look happy in these pictures, Ketch. Do you know why? It's because after you take away the religious trappings of holidays like this, and the commercialism, what's left is family. And you were with your family."

"I have no family now," he croaked. "You took that away from me, in case you forgot."

"Is that what you think?" She cocked her head at him. "I had my faults, of course – but you didn't understand me, Ketch, and you didn't understand our son. You didn't know what we needed, because you didn't know what *you* needed. You were always working toward some future point in time when everything would align and your world would be perfect. You were waiting until then to allow yourself to be truly happy, and while you worked and waited, you pushed us farther and farther away."

He fidgeted uncomfortably in his seat. He didn't know what to say.

"But Ketch," she continued, "the thing is, that time never comes. It's just a carrot that dangles in front of you, always out of reach, to make you keep racing. Instead of chasing that carrot, you need to make the most of each day as it comes."

He realized he couldn't argue with her. As painful as the admission was, he knew everything she was saying was true. He sighed, and she waited patiently for him to catch up.

"When did you get so wise?" he finally said, with a hint of a rueful smile.

She laughed again. "I don't know, but it sure took me long enough, didn't it?" Then she got serious again. "It can happen to you, too, Ketch, if you let it."

"Why did you come here?" he asked again.

"I wanted you to know some things," she answered, "before it's too late."

"Too late for what?"

She just smiled. "I wanted you to know that old wounds can be healed, you can make new friends, and family can be anyone if you let them know you well enough." She returned the album to her purse and glanced around the room. "I need to find the facilities. Go make a friend while I'm gone." She rose from her seat and placed a hand on his shoulder. "You can be happy again, Ketch," she said, and then she bustled off.

Somehow Ketch knew she wouldn't be coming back. He looked down at Jack and saw that the dog's eyes were now open. "Well, she's gone," he said. "Why didn't you say hello?" Jack's eyes started to close again. Say hello to whom, Ketch imagined he might have asked if he could talk.

It looked like some among the crowd in the hall were done eating and starting to dance. He finished his beer and decided to get another to wash his probably cold dinner down with. "I'll be right back, boy," he said to the dog. "You stay here and be good."

He left the dog leashed to the chair and wended his way through the dancers to the drink table. When he turned to leave the table, full cup in hand, a woman accidently jostled his elbow and made him spill some of his beer.

"Lordy, I am *so* sorry!" she exclaimed. "Are you okay? Did you get all wet?"

Ordinarily, her clumsiness might have annoyed him. But he felt different now than he had yesterday. "Oh, just my hand – and my sneakers, I think," he replied, looking himself over. He smiled at her. "But they'll live. They've seen worse."

"Well, you come on over here," she said, leading him to one end of the table, "and I'll get you some napkins and some more beer. There you go. You just stay put now, hear?" Ketch set his half-empty cup – or half-full, depending on one's outlook – on the table and shook some beer from his hand.

She returned shortly, with napkins and two more cups. "I got one for myself, too," she said. She set the cups down and passed him a wad of napkins. "Here you go. There's some wet wipes in there, too."

"Thank you," Ketch said.

"No, thank *you* for not rippin' me a new one!" She drank some of her beer while Ketch cleaned himself up. "So Ketch," she said when he was through, "are you on vacation again, or are you finally doin' the deed and stayin' here for good?"

Ketch was taken aback. How did she know his name, for starters? And what his plans were? He took a closer look at her. Slender but muscular, auburn pony tail, green eyes, mid-thirties maybe... He didn't know her name, but she did seem familiar to him.

"I'm sorry, but do I know you?" he asked.

"You stopped by my shop one time last year. The Sea Dog Scuba Center, in Avon?"

She was right. He remembered the place now, a nondescript old wooden building just off the highway on the north end of town. But had he told her his name, or that he'd been thinking of moving to Avon?

"Oh, yes, I did stop there once," he said, and let the rest go for now. He also diplomatically refrained from mentioning that in past years he'd patronized a competitor of hers down in Hatteras village when he'd wanted to go diving.

"You know, you don't have to go all the way to Hatteras when you want to dive," she said, making him do another double-take. It was as if she'd read his mind. "I hooked up with a charter captain over at the

Kinnakeet Boatyard. He's a good old boy. With just a twelve-pack and a compass, he'll you take anywhere he can!" She laughed at her own joke.

Ketch politely smiled, then said, "Well, I am in fact moving to Avon. I just arrived this week."

"No kiddin'! Where're you stayin' at?"

"I rented a place in Buxton until I can find a house to buy."

"Well hey, I live in Buxton! I have an apartment there."

"How about that?" Ketch picked up both of his cups. "Well, I brought my dog with me, and I should get back to him, so..."

"Oh, that's your dog over there? I have one, too, but he's back home. He's gettin' pretty old now, and he was too tired to come. So okay, let's go. Mind if I set with y'all? We ought to talk some more. I might could help you out."

There were more dancers out on the floor now, but they were able to make their way through the crowd without spilling any more beer. The dog acknowledged the presence of the woman this time, standing and wagging as they approached. Or was he just wagging at his master, Ketch wondered?

"Well hey there, you!" she said to the dog. "What's his name?"

"That's Jack."

"Hey, Jack! Good boy!"

They sat down, and she talked while Ketch ate. Jack lay next to Ketch again. He stayed awake this time, though, in case of a handout.

In short order, Ketch learned there was a house for sale on the sound near that old boatyard that might be just perfect for him, and that it was reasonably priced (relatively speaking, as waterfront property was never cheap these days). He also learned the winter hours for her shop in case he wanted to come by sometime, and a little more about the semi-retired captain who docked at the boatyard.

"But he hadn't got back from Florida yet, that I know of," she was saying. "He goes there in the winter and doesn't come back here 'til springtime, but I called him on Christmas and he said he was sailin' back early this year on account of some family thing he's got goin' on. He's got a condo in Hatteras. Anyway, I bet you and him would get on just fine."

"I imagine so," Ketch said, wiping his mouth.

"You know," she said, "Mama was kinda disappointed when you didn't show for Christmas dinner. But she made a right nice toast to you anyway."

"What?" he said. What was she talking about?

"Hey, you done eatin'?" she asked. Without waiting for an answer, she jumped up and said, "Come on, let's go outside and get some of those oysters. I could use some fresh air, and I bet Jack might could use a break, right? And I want to check on Timmy."

"Okay," he said, playing along and untying Jack's leash from his chair. It had certainly been a strange day so far. Could it get any stranger? "Come on boy, let's go out. Who's Timmy?" he asked on the way.

"Oh, he's that kid that was hitchin' out on 12

before. You know, the one you didn't stop for?" Ketch didn't know what to say to that. Had she been behind him on his way up here? "Well, I picked him up, and I'll take him back with me later on." It was dark now, and she stopped at a strategic vantage point to scan the grounds. "I hope he got himself somethin' to eat. I paid his way in."

"Why?" Ketch asked.

"'Cause it's Christmas, silly! Some folks aren't as fortunate as me'n you, you know. He lives with his grand-dad in an old shack down at the end of my road, and they don't have much. The old man fishes, mostly for mullet, and Timmy does what he can to help out. You might see him ridin' his pony sometime, lookin' for bottles and cans to turn in. He thought he might could pick up a bunch of 'em around here today."

"I guess I could have picked him up and helped him out," he said. He felt bad now about not having done so.

"Why? Aren't there programs and charities for folks like them?" she replied with just a hint of acid in her voice.

But that isn't enough, Ketch thought. "He sounds like Taffy," he observed.

"Huh? Who's that?"

"The main character in a novel for young readers, *Taffy of Torpedo Junction*. It's said to be a classic in these parts."

"Oh yeah, I read that, a long time ago."

"Isn't it dangerous for him to hitchhike? He

couldn't be more than twelve, maybe even ten."

"I know he doesn't look it, but he's fourteen. But yeah, it's still dangerous, and I spoke to him about that. I called his grand-dad, too, to let him know what was goin' on. Oh, there he is. Hey Timmy!" The boy waved back, and they joined him at one of the oyster-covered tables.

"Timmy, this is Ketch," the woman said. "How'd you make out?"

"Pretty darn good, ma'am! I stuck two big bags in the back of your car, like you said, next to your cooler. Here's your keys back. Nice to meet you, sir," the boy said. Ketch nodded at him.

"Thanks, Timmy," she said. "You locked it back up, right? Don't want somebody takin' my oysters!" she explained to Ketch.

"Why do you have oysters?" he asked.

"Oh, I won me a bag in the oyster shoot. Well, not exactly," she laughed. "I entered every round'n lost every dang one of 'em. But they felt sorry for me and gave me a bag anyway at the end, for effort I guess."

She'd been here for the oyster shoot? But that had been over with when he and Jack had arrived, and she had to have picked up the boy after he'd passed him by.

Before he could give that some more thought, his cell phone alerted him of an incoming message, a rare event for him these days. "Excuse me," he said, "I should probably see what this is." He stepped away from the table and left the woman and the boy to munch on roasted oysters.

The caller ID didn't say where the message had come from. And there was no text in the message, just some attached photos. He tapped on the icon and watched.

He pieced together the story from a progression of grainy black-and-white shots. It began with a rather startling and gruesome image. Someone had died in a grubby room somewhere, and from the looks of the body, it hadn't been found for some time. There was a dried-up Christmas wreath hanging on the wall. The police and a coroner were called and the body was transported to a morgue. After a cursory autopsy, the body was taken to a funeral home and cremated. The ashes were then scooped into a cardboard box, which was driven to a cemetery and buried without ceremony. There was no service of any kind, and there was no one at the grave but the workers. Finally, a simple wooden marker was stuck into the freshly turned ground.

There was a name on the marker, and two dates with a dash between them. He couldn't quite make them out, so he zoomed in on the marker. It was fuzzy, but now he could decipher the first date – which as it turned out happened to be his own birthday. The other date was past the edge of the screen. With a strong sense of foreboding, he scrolled up until the date was gone and he could see part of the name.

The first name of the deceased was 'Storm'. He blinked a couple of times and looked again, and it still read the same. He scrolled right far enough to see that the surname was indeed 'Ketchum'.

He felt as though he'd been punched in the chest. Was all this supposed to represent some future Christmas of his? If so, it was apparently a time when he was completely alone in the world, and there was no one at all to care whether he lived or died. Was this meant to be some kind of warning about what awaited him down the line if he didn't change his ways?

He resumed breathing. Who would send him something like this? And why? This was beyond cruel. He found himself tempted to scroll down to read the other date, but he decided to turn the phone off instead. Though it was probably just a prank, he didn't want to know, just in case.

There was some sort of commotion now over by the oyster tables. When he turned to see what was going on, he beheld a monstrous-looking apparition lurching along between the tables, occasionally bumping into them as well as any people who got in its way.

"It's Old Buck!" someone shouted. "Can't be, *I'm* Old Buck!" another voice called back. But it did indeed look like Old Buck, except that there appeared to be only one person under the blanket instead of the usual two Ketch remembered reading about. And this Old Buck was early, and he was in the wrong place.

Ketch knew about the legend of Old Buck, a bull that had purportedly come ashore from a shipwreck and run wild on the island back in the eighteen hundreds, when there'd been cattle here. In addition to terrorizing the island folk until he was finally shot, it was said that he'd impregnated every cow on the island during his rampage. His spirit was reputed to live on in Trent Woods, the southern end of Buxton Woods, and now he traditionally visits Rodanthe at Old Christmas each year – in the form of a bull skull on a wood frame supported by one or two men and covered with a blanket. The twenty-fifth was for Santa and church; today was Old Buck's day, and his appearance was the highlight of the celebration.

But if Ketch remembered right from his reading, Old Buck wasn't supposed to make his entrance until at least nine o'clock, and he was supposed to appear in the dance hall. Ketch watched until the legendary bull disappeared around the corner of the community building.

"The cash box, where's the cash box?" one of the women manning the cash table started demanding of anyone who'd listen. "It's gone, where is it?" she wailed.

Some of the men went to her, and some others ran around the corner of the building where Old Buck had last been seen. Those men returned with just the skull and the blanket.

Two Dare County sheriff's deputies had stationed themselves in the parking lot a while earlier, probably in case any brawls broke out, Ketch thought. After drinking all afternoon and into the evening, it had also become somewhat of a tradition at this event for some of the local fishermen to settle any differences they might have had during the previous year through fisticuffs. But there hadn't been any such occurrences so far today. The deputies briefly conferred with the people at the cash table, and then one returned to their cruiser and got on the radio while the other retraced the route the ersatz Old Buck had taken.

Timmy and the woman from the dive shop rejoined him then. Ketch still didn't know her name, and he kept forgetting to ask her for it.

"Somebody up and stole the cashbox," she said.

"So I heard," Ketch said. "I'm thinking it may have been two people working together. That Old Buck act was probably a diversion so the other one could make off with the cashbox."

"That's what they think, too. Hey, you're pretty good at this!"

"But who would do that?" Ketch asked. "I thought you pretty much all knew one another here."

"Yeah, we mostly do, but we always get some outsiders. Some folks come over from the mainland, and some drive down from up the beach."

"Has anyone driven anything out of here since this happened?"

"They don't think so, but the robbers could have parked a getaway car out by the road. They're gonna block off the lot for a while so nobody can leave. The sheriff's office is sendin' a cruiser down from Manteo to watch the bridge at Oregon Inlet, and they're gonna watch the ferry docks in Hatteras. Those are the only ways to drive off the island."

"Well, that won't help if they don't leave the island right away, or if they've got themselves a boat," Timmy contributed.

"That's true, Timmy," Ketch said. "But what if they didn't go anywhere? What if they're still here?"

"What do you mean?" the woman asked.

"Well, if I were the one trying to steal that box, I don't think I'd just run off with it. I could get caught that way. I'd probably hide it somewhere and come back for it later after everyone's gone, or at least wait until they gave up on looking for it. And if that's what's happening here," he mused, "the next question is, where might they have hidden it?"

"Well, I don't rightly know – but your dog might could find it," Timmy interjected.

"That's right!" the woman said. "I know he's not a police dog or a bloodhound, but you said he's real smart, right? Let's put him on the case!"

Had he said that? But it was true that Jack was probably the smartest dog he'd ever known. Ketch took his wallet out of his pocket.

"I don't think this will work," he said, "but I guess it's worth a try." He led Jack to the table the cashbox had rested on. The crowd there was dispersing, and no one questioned what they might be doing. The dog sniffed around the table some, and then Ketch pulled some bills from his wallet and let the dog sniff them as well.

"Now remember, we don't want to tip our hand, in case they're watching. Just act like we're taking Jack for a walk," Ketch directed the other two. Then he crouched by the dog. "Find it," he discreetly commanded him. "Find the money." He let the dog off the leash. "Go on, boy."

Jack seemed to understand what was expected of him. Nose to the ground, he meandered around the table for a minute or so, then set off on a deliberate path along the side of the building. Ketch wondered if the dog was tracking the scent of the money, or if he'd picked up on something else?

Ketch didn't think it would be possible to hide anything under the community building, especially if one were in a hurry. There wasn't that much space under the building, and the slats nailed across the pilings would preclude easy access to the crawlspace. Sure enough, Jack continued on past the building to a nearby structure that appeared to be some kind of gift shop. This building had more freeboard and no slats between its pilings. The dog ducked under the building, and a moment later Ketch heard him give a little yip.

"I think he found it!" Timmy stage-whispered. He wanted to go to the dog, but Ketch stopped him. He quietly called Jack back and leashed him.

"Good boy, Jack, good boy!" Ketch praised the dog. He scratched him behind both ears at the same time, something Ketch knew he especially enjoyed.

"But don't we want to go get that box?" Timmy asked.

"No," Ketch answered. "Keep walking."

"What are you up to, Ketch?" the woman asked.

"I think we should set a trap. Then we can return the money and catch the thieves as well."

Ketch led the group on around the perimeter of the community building, and laid out his plan while they walked. When they'd returned to their starting point, he sent Timmy back alone to verify what Jack had found under the building. In the meantime, he finally tried a roasted oyster. It wasn't bad, he decided, but nothing to write home about. He still preferred his shrimp and crab cakes.

When they next saw Timmy, Ketch could tell the boy was consciously working at controlling his excitement.

"It's there, all right!" he said. "Behind a pilin', under some sand and eel grass."

"Good work, Timmy," Ketch's other new friend said. That's right, he'd made not just one, as he'd been instructed, but two so far. Thinking of the pictures on his phone, he wondered if that would earn him any points.

"I'll go have a talk with the deputies," she continued. "I know one of 'em. Maybe they can get most of these people back inside and set up a little ole stakeout. Then maybe those robbers'll get cocky enough to go for that box."

Ketch, Jack, and Timmy went inside while she went off to speak with the deputies. "Did you get any supper?" he asked the boy.

"Yes sir, I did. But I hadn't made it to the dessert table yet."

"Well then, let's go check that out and see what they have," Ketch said with a smile. The boy still looked only about as clean as he had out on the road earlier, but there was more to him than met the eye, Ketch now knew. He found he was pleased rather than embarrassed by the boy tagging along with him.

The woman rejoined them after they'd found a place to sit, carrying two more cups of beer and a soft drink. "Well, it's all set. Now we just have to wait," she said.

They ate and drank and talked as the hall filled with people. There were more dancers now than ever, and Ketch was glad he'd found their seats when he had. He was also relieved that the woman didn't seem interested in dancing, something he wasn't especially fond of doing himself.

It wasn't too much longer before they were approached by two men, one of the deputies and someone from the staff of the community building. The scoundrels who'd hidden the cashbox had indeed gotten cocky, and they were now in custody.

"Thank you so much!" the staffer said to the woman. "Is there anything we can do for you in return? You want some oysters to take home?"

"Oh, I didn't do much," she said. "It was Ketch had the idea of the box bein' hidden, and to set that trap. Besides, I already got me a bag of oysters at the shoot."

"Well, how about a bag for me, and one of those delicious pies?" Ketch said. "And two chicken stews to go?" He stopped then, his face reddening. "I'm sorry, is that too much?"

The staffer laughed. "Surely not, it's the least we can do! I'll have somebody box up that pie and stew for you, and I'll send word down that you'll be pickin' up some oysters."

"And then I think I should get Timmy on home," the woman said.

"But you're gonna miss Old Buck, then," the staffer warned.

"Oh well! Been there, done that," she laughed. Timmy went off with the staffer, so he could carry the box back. When he was out of earshot, the woman regarded Ketch with a new kind of interest.

"I thought you said you didn't like pecan pie," she said. "Nor those oysters all that much neither."

"Timmy and his grandfather will like them. It's all going to their place, if you don't mind carting it there for me."

"I thought so," she said, "and I don't mind one bit. It'll make a fine Sunday dinner for them, a lot finer than they're used to." She looked up at him approvingly. "So, you gonna stay for Old Buck? The real one, I mean?"

"Yes, I think I will. I haven't been there and done that yet."

"All right then. Say, seems like you might be good at solvin' mysteries," she said with a twinkle in her eye. "You ever thought about bein' a private eye? Since you're retired now, you could hang a shingle and see what happens. It'd give you somethin' to do."

Well, he didn't know about that. And had he said he was retired? He didn't think so.

"Anyway, here comes Timmy now. Hey, don't be a stranger, hear? Come on by the shop sometime. And don't forget to bring my Jacky-boy!" she smiled.

"I will, I promise," he said, and meant it.

After she and Timmy had left, he sat back down, drew the dog to him, and gave him a big hug. "You're the best dog I ever had," he told him – which Jack apparently appreciated, as he started licking the man's face and ears and neck, and kept licking, and licking...

~ ~ ~

And licking, though it was actually Ketch's hand and arm. He woke with a start and sat up straight in the rocking chair.

"Jack?" he said. He looked around in puzzlement at the initially unfamiliar landscape that surrounded him. The sun was fully up now, but he could tell it was still early. He must have dozed off for a little while.

"What is it, boy? Was I talking in my sleep? It's okay, I'm okay now." He petted and reassured the dog, settled back in the rocker, and tried to think.

Though it was already dissipating, as his dreams always did, he focused hard and managed to retain considerably more of it than he was typically able to before it could completely slip away – enough to acknowledge that he'd probably owe Dickens a nod if the man were still living. And enough to be reminded and cognizant of the spirits' lesson therein.

This one had been a dilly, for sure. Was Timmy real, he wondered? His ex-wife, of course, was a real person, and so was that woman from the dive shop. He'd stopped in there once a while back, and he remembered seeing her there. Well, if he ever did encounter a boy like that around here, he resolved to not just arbitrarily ignore him as he might have before. In fact, if he saw anyone like that up in Rodanthe later, he might pay their way in to the Old Christmas celebration if it looked like they needed someone to.

Ketch rose from the chair and stretched, then went back inside the cottage to the kitchen. He bagged all the liquor bottles but one and tossed them in the big black trash barrel outside. Now that he was finally where his soul had longed to be, it wouldn't do to drink that away. He kept the few beers that remained, though, and a lone bottle of tequila, in case he got in a parrothead mood sometime. He didn't think he needed to get *too* monkish.

Then he went to the bathroom to shave and shower. Yes, he and Jack would drive up to Rodanthe today after all, so he guessed he should try to look presentable.

He realized he didn't really want to lead the solitary life of a monk or hermit. As Mister Buffett had once sung about a friend of his, some of it was magic and some of it was tragic, but he'd had a good life at one time and it could be good again. Although this particular pirate was looking at fifty-five rather than forty, he decided to take the view from now on that any day he wasn't six feet under was a good day.

When they were ready to head out, he thought maybe they'd drop by that pleasantly bohemian boatyard first and see if there was anyone around who might want to join them in Rodanthe. That place was real, too, and he knew where it was, and he'd spoken to a couple of people there in the past. And while he was in that neighborhood, he could take a quick look around and see if there happened to be a soundfront house for sale somewhere around there. That would be something, if there was, though he wasn't superstitious enough to think it would mean anything.

All told, it might not seem like much to most. But it was a plan, and it was what he could do today. And it was a start.

~ The End ~

Thanks for reading this story! I hope you enjoyed it. If you did, keep a weather eye out for the next Storm Ketchum tale! You might also enjoy Ketch's full-length adventures, if you haven't already read them:

If you have time, please consider taking a few minutes to log a review. Reviews help increase an independently published book's visibility, and I'd greatly appreciate it. Thanks again!

Made in the USA
Middletown, DE
09 August 2015